THE
SECRET
GARDEN

Abridged from the original by
Frances Hodgson Burnett

Illustrations by
Hae Ran Lee

CD *narrated by*
Jenny Agutter

SOURCEBOOKS
Jabberwocky
AN IMPRINT OF SOURCEBOOKS

Published by Sourcebooks Jabberwocky, an imprint of Sourcebooks, Inc.
P.O. Box 4410, Naperville, Illinois 60567-4410
(630) 961-3900
Fax: (630) 961-2168
www.sourcebooks.com

Library of Congress Cataloging-in-Publication Data

Burnett, Frances Hodgson.
  The secret garden / abridged from the original by Frances Hodgson Burnett ; illustrations by
Hae Ran Lee.
      p. cm.
  Summary: Ten-year-old Mary comes to live in a lonely house on the Yorkshire moors and dis-
covers an invalid cousin and the mysteries of a locked garden.
  [1. Orphans--Fiction. 2. Gardens--Fiction. 3. People with disabilities--Fiction 4. Yorkshire
(England)--History--20th century--Fiction. 5. Great Britain--History--Edward VII, 1901-1910-
-Fiction.] I. Lee, Hae Ran, ill. II. Title.

PZ7.B934Se 2007
[Fic]--dc22

                    2007022755
                 Printed in China.
                 OGP 10 9 8 7

Source of Production: O.G. Printing Productions, Ltd. Kowloon, Hong Kong
Date of Production: February 2012
ID # 17166

CONTENTS

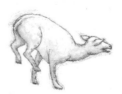

Chapter 1

THERE IS NO ONE LEFT

When Mary Lennox was sent to Misselthwaite Manor to live with her uncle everybody said she was the most disagreeable-looking child ever seen. It was true, too. Her hair was yellow, and her face was yellow because she had been born in India and had always been ill in one way or another. Her father had held a

position under the English Government and her mother had been a great beauty who only cared to go to parties. She had not wanted a little girl at all, and when Mary was born she handed her over to the care of an Ayah, a servant, to keep the sickly, fretful thing out of the way.

One hot morning, when she was nine years old, she awakened feeling cross, and she became crosser still when she saw that the servant who stood by her bedside was not her Ayah.

"Send my Ayah to me."

The woman looked frightened, but only stammered that the Ayah could not come and when Mary threw herself into a passion, she looked only more frightened and repeated that it was not possible for the Ayah to come to Missie Sahib.

The cholera had broken
out in its most fatal form.
The Ayah had been taken
ill in the night, and had
just died. Before the
next day three other
servants were dead and
others had run away in
terror. There was panic
on every side, and during
the confusion Mary hid
herself in the nursery
and was forgotten.
She could scarcely
keep her eyes
open and

she lay down on her bed and knew nothing more for a long time.

When she awakened she lay and stared at the wall. The house was perfectly still.

The next minute she heard footsteps in the compound, and then on the veranda. They were men's footsteps.

Mary was standing in the middle of the nursery when they opened the door.

"Mercy on us, who is she!"

"I am Mary Lennox. Why does nobody come?"

"Poor little kid!" he said. "There is nobody left to come."

Mary was very young, and as she had always been taken care of, she supposed she always would be. She knew that she was not going to stay at the English clergyman's house where she was taken at first. The clergyman had five children nearly all the same age.

By the second day they had given her a nick-name; it was Basil who thought of it. Basil was a little boy with impudent blue eyes and a turned-up nose, and Mary hated him.

Basil called Mary "Mistress Mary, quite contrary" and
the children would taunt her with the nursery rhyme:

> Mistress Mary, quite contrary
> How does your garden grow?
> With silver bells and cockle shells
> And marigolds all in a row.

"You are going to be sent home," Basil said to her,
"at the end of the week. And we're glad of it."

"I am glad of it, too," answered Mary.

"She doesn't know where home is!" said Basil.

"It's England, of course. You are going to your uncle.
His name is Mr. Archibald Craven. He lives in a great,
big, old house, and no one goes near him. He's so cross
he won't let them."

"I don't believe you," said Mary

Mary made the long voyage to England under the

care of an officer's wife. She was very much absorbed in her own little boy and girl, and was rather glad to hand the child over to the woman Mr. Archibald Craven sent to meet her, in London. The woman was his house-keeper, Mrs. Medlock. She was a stout woman, with very red cheeks and sharp black eyes. Mary thought Mrs. Medlock the most disagreeable person she had ever seen, with her common face and her common bon-net. When the next day they set out on their journey to Yorkshire, she walked through the station trying to keep as far away from her as she could, because she did not want to seem to belong to her.

Mary sat in her corner of the railway carriage and looked plain and fretful. Mrs. Medlock had never seen a child who sat so still without doing anything.

"Do you know anything about your uncle?"

"No," said Mary.

"I suppose you might as well be told something—to prepare you. The house is six hundred years old and it's on the edge of a moor, and there's near a hundred rooms in it, though most of them's shut up and locked. He's not going to trouble himself about you, that's sure and certain. He never troubles himself about no one. He's got a crooked back— that set him wrong. He was a sour young man— till he was married. She was a sweet, pretty thing. Nobody thought she'd marry him, but she did. And when she died—"

"Oh! Did she die!"

"Yes, she died. And it made him queerer than ever. Most of the time he goes away, and when he is at Misselthwaite he shuts himself up in the West Wing. There's gardens enough.

But when you're in the house don't go wandering and poking about."

"I shall not want to go poking about," said sour little Mary.

The station was a small one and nobody but themselves seemed to be getting out of the train. On the road was a smart carriage, and a smart footman helped her in. He shut the door, and they drove off.

At last they stopped before an immensely long house which seemed to ramble round a stone court. A thin old man stood near the manservant who opened the door for them. And then Mary Lennox was led up a broad staircase and down a long corridor and up a short flight of steps, until a door opened in a wall and she found herself in a room with a fire in it and a supper on the table.

Chapter 2

MARTHA

When she opened her eyes in the morning it was because a young housemaid had come into her room to light the fire.

"That's th' moor. Does tha' like it?"

Everyone at Misselthwaite spoke in a broad fashion which Mary found out afterward was Yorkshire. They would say "thou" instead of "you" but then shorten it to "tha'," and shorten many other words.

"No, I hate it."

"It's fair lovely in the spring an' summer when th' gorse an' broom an' heather's in flower."

Mary listened to her. The servants in India were not like this.

"You are a strange servant."

Martha sat up on her heels, and laughed.

"You wrap up warm an' run out an' play," said Martha. "It'll do you good."

"Out? Why should I go out on a day like this? Who will go with me?"

"You'll go by yourself. Our Dickon goes

off on th' moor by himself an' plays for hours. That's how he made friends with th' pony, an' birds as comes an' eats out of his hand. If tha' goes round that way tha'll come to th' gardens," she said, pointing to a gate in a wall of shrubbery. One of th' gardens is locked up. No one has been in it for ten years."

"Why?" asked Mary.

"Mr. Craven had it shut when his wife died so sudden. He won't let no one go inside. It was her garden. He locked th' door an' dug a hole and buried th' key."

Mary turned down the walk, and through the shrubbery gate she found herself in great gardens, with wide lawns and trees, and evergreens clipped into strange shapes, and a large pool with an old grey fountain. But the flower-beds were bare and the fountain was not playing.

At the end of the path she was following, there seemed to be a long wall, with ivy growing over it. There was a green door in the ivy, and it stood open. She went through the door and found that it was one of several walled gardens which seemed to open into one another.

Presently an old man with a spade over his shoulder walked through the door. He looked startled when he saw Mary. He had a surly old face, and did not seem at all pleased to see her.

"What is this place?" she asked.

"One o' th' kitchen-gardens."

"What is that?" said Mary, pointing through the other green door.

"Another of 'em. There's another on t'other side o' th' wall an' there's th' orchard on t'other side o' that."

"Can I go in them?"

"If tha' likes."

Mary went down the path and through the second green door. But in the second wall there was another green door and it was not open. Perhaps it led into the garden which no one had seen for ten years. She went to the green door and turned the handle. She hoped the door would not open—but it did, and she found herself in an orchard. There were walls all round it also but there was no green door anywhere. She could see the tops of trees above the wall, and when she stood still she saw a bird with a bright red breast sitting on the topmost branch of one of them, and suddenly he burst into his winter song.

She stopped and listened and the bright-breasted little bird brought a look into her sour little face which was almost a smile.

Why had Mr. Archibald Craven buried the key? If he had liked his wife so much why did he hate her garden? If she should ever see him, she knew that she would not like him, and he would not like her.

"People never like me and I never like people," she thought.

She thought of the robin.

"I believe that tree was in the secret garden. There was a wall round the place and no door."

She walked back into the first kitchen-garden and found the old man digging.

"There was no door there into the other garden."

"What garden?" he said.

"The one on the other side of the wall," answered Mistress Mary. "There are trees there. A bird with a red breast was sitting on one of them and he sang."

To her surprise the surly old weather-beaten face actually changed its expression. A slow smile spread over it.

He began to whistle—a low soft whistle. Almost the next moment she heard a soft little rushing flight through the air—it was the bird with the red breast, and he alighted quite near to the gardener's foot.

"Where has tha' been, tha' cheeky little beggar?" he said.

The bird put his tiny head on one side and looked up at him with his soft bright eye. He hopped about and pecked the earth briskly. It actually gave Mary a queer feeling in her heart—he was so pretty and cheerful.

"Will he always come when you call him?"

"Aye, he will. I've knowed him ever since he was a fledgling."

"What kind of a bird is he?"

"Doesn't tha' know? He's a robin redbreast."

She went a step nearer to the robin and looked at him very hard. "I'm lonely," she said.

The old gardener pushed his hat back on his head.

"What is your name?" Mary inquired.

"Ben Weatherstaff, I'm lonely mysel' except when he's with me, he's th' only friend I've got."

Suddenly a clear rippling little sound broke out near her and she turned round. Ben Weatherstaff laughed.

"Dang me if he hasn't taken a fancy to thee."

"To me?" said Mary, and she moved towards the little tree softly and looked up. "Would you make friends with me?"

"Why, tha' said that almost like Dickon talks to his wild things on th' moor."

"Do you know Dickon?" Mary asked.

"Everybody knows him. I'll warrant th' foxes shows him where their cubs lies an' th' skylarks don't hide their nests from him."

Mary would have liked to ask some more questions. But just at that moment the robin gave a little shake of his wings, and flew away.

"He has flown into the garden where there is no door!"

"He lives there."

"Where is the green door? There must be a door somewhere."

"There was ten years ago, but there isn't now."

"No door! There must be."

"None as anyone can find."

And he stopped digging, and walked off.

Chapter 3

THE CRY IN THE CORRIDOR

At first each day for Mary Lennox was exactly like the others. Every morning she realized that if she did not go out she would have to stay in and do nothing—and so she went out.

One place she went to oftener than to any other was the long walk outside the gardens. Against the walls ivy grew thickly. There was one part of the wall where the creeping dark green leaves were more bushy than elsewhere.

A few days after she had talked to Ben Weatherstaff, Mary stopped to notice this, and there, on top of the wall, perched Ben Weatherstaff's robin redbreast.

"Oh!" she cried out, "is it you?"

A robin frequently visited Frances Hodgson Burnett when she was writing in her garden. She later wrote a book entitled *My Robin*, in answer to a reader's question about the robin in *The Secret Garden*.

He twittered and chirped and hopped along the wall as if he were telling her all sorts of things. Mary began to laugh, and as he hopped and took little flights along the wall she ran after him.

"I like you!" she cried out.

He made a darting flight to the top of a tree, where he reminded Mary of the first time she had seen him. He had been on a tree-top then and she had been in the orchard.

She walked round and looked closely at that side of the orchard wall. Then she ran through the kitchen-gardens again and out into the walk outside the long ivy-covered wall, and she walked to the end of it and then to the other end.

"It's very queer," she said. "Ben Weatherstaff said there was no door. But there must have been one ten years ago, because Mr. Craven buried the key."

She stayed out of doors nearly all day, and when she sat down to her supper at night she felt hungry and drowsy and comfortable. She did not feel cross when Martha chattered away, and at last she thought she would ask her a question.

"Why did Mr. Craven hate the garden?"

"It was Mrs. Craven's garden that she had made when first they were married an' she just loved it. An' there was an old tree with a branch bent like a seat on it, an' she used to sit there. But one day th' branch broke an' she fell on th' ground an' was hurt so bad that next day she died. That's why he hates it."

Mary did not ask any more questions; she looked at the red fire and listened to the wind "wutherin'" louder than ever. But as she was listening she began to listen to something else, a sound as if a child were crying. Sometimes the wind sounded like a child crying, but Mary felt sure this sound was inside the house.

"Wuthering" is how the people of Yorkshire describe the sound of the wind rushing around a house like someone trying to break in. *Wuthering Heights* is a famous novel about another manor on the Yorkshire moors.

"Do you hear anyone crying?" she said.

"No. It's th' wind."

"But listen. It's in the house."

And at that very moment a door must have been opened somewhere downstairs, for a great rushing

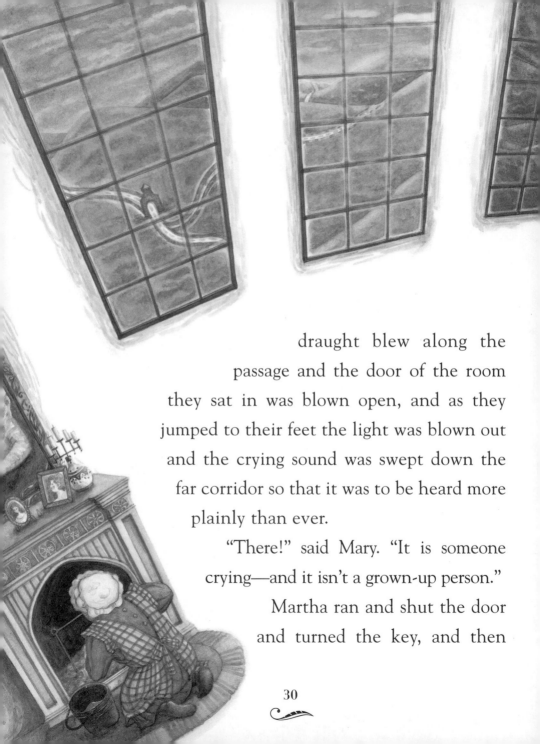

draught blew along the passage and the door of the room they sat in was blown open, and as they jumped to their feet the light was blown out and the crying sound was swept down the far corridor so that it was to be heard more plainly than ever.

"There!" said Mary. "It is someone crying—and it isn't a grown-up person."

Martha ran and shut the door and turned the key, and then

everything was quiet.

The next day the rain poured down
again, and when Mary looked out of her window
the moor was almost hidden by grey mist and cloud.

"What do you do in your cottage when it rains like
this?" she asked Martha.

"Try to keep from under each other's feet mostly,"
Martha answered. "Dickon he doesn't mind th' wet. He
says he sees things on rainy days as doesn't show when
it's fair weather. He once found a little fox cub half
drowned in its hole. He's got it at home now. He found

a half-drowned crow another time an' he brought it home, too, an' it hops an' flies about with him everywhere."

"If I had a raven or a fox cub I could play with it," said Mary. "But I have nothing."

Martha looked perplexed. "Can tha' knit?" she asked.

"No," answered Mary.

"Can tha' sew?"

"No."

"Can tha' read?"

"Yes."

"Then why doesn't tha' read somethin'?"

"I haven't any books."

"If Mrs. Medlock'd let thee go into th' library, there's thousands o' books there."

Mary made up her mind to go and find it herself. She wandered about long enough to feel too tired to wander any further, and at last she reached her own floor again, though she was some distance from her own room and did not know exactly where she was, standing still at

what seemed the end of a short passage with tapestry on the wall.

It was while she was standing here that the stillness was broken by a fretful childish whine. Her heart beating rather faster, she put her hand upon the tapestry near her, and then sprang back. The tapestry was the covering of a door which fell open and showed another part of the corridor behind it, and Mrs. Medlock coming up it with her bunch of keys in her hand.

"What are you doing here?"

"I turned the wrong corner. I didn't know which way to go and I heard someone crying."

"You didn't hear anything of the sort."

And she took her by the arm and half pushed, half pulled her up one passage and down another until she pushed her in at the door of her own room.

Chapter 4

THE KEY OF THE GARDEN

T wo days after this, when Mary opened her eyes she sat upright in bed immediately.

"Look at the moor!"

The rainstorm had ended and a brilliant, deep blue sky arched high over the moorland.

"Aye," said Martha. "Th' springtime's on its way."

She went away in high spirits as soon as she had given Mary her breakfast, and Mary felt lonelier than ever. She went out into the garden as quickly as possible. She went first into the kitchen-garden and found Ben Weatherstaff working there with two other gardeners. "Springtime's comin,'" he said. "Cannot tha' smell it?"

Mary sniffed.

"That's th' good rich earth. It's in a good humor makin' ready to grow things."

Very soon she heard the soft rustling flight of the robin. He hopped about close to her feet, and put his head on one side and looked at her slyly.

"Do you think he remembers me?"

"Remembers thee! He's never seen a little wench here before, an' he's bent on findin' out all about thee."

She heard a chirp and a twitter, and when she looked at the bare flower-bed at her left side there he was hopping about.

"You do remember me!" she cried out. "You do! You are prettier than anything else in the world!"

The flower-bed was bare of flowers, but there were shrubs at the back, and as the robin hopped about under them she saw him hop over something almost buried in the soil. It was a ring of rusty iron or brass and when the robin flew up into a tree nearby she picked the ring up. It was more than a ring, however; it was an old key.

She looked at the key quite a long time, and thought about the closed garden. It was because it had been shut up so long that she wanted to see it. Besides that, if she liked it she could go into it every day and shut the door behind her, and nobody would ever know where she was, but would think the door was still locked and the key buried in the earth.

"Perhaps it has been buried for ten years!" said Mary. "Perhaps it is the key to the garden!" She made up her mind that she should always carry it with her, so that if she should ever find the hidden garden she would be ready.

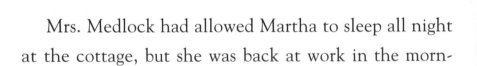

Mrs. Medlock had allowed Martha to sleep all night at the cottage, but she was back at work in the morning, and was full of stories of her day out.

"I've brought thee a present."

"A present!"

She brought it out from under her apron. It was a strong, slender rope with a striped red and blue handle at each end.

"What is it for?"

"For! This is what it's for."

And she began to skip.

"It looks nice. Do you think I could ever skip like that?"

"You just try it."

"Martha, thank you."

The sun was shining and a little wind was blowing in delightful little gusts.

Mary skipped round all the gardens and round the orchard.

She stopped with a little laugh of pleasure, and there, lo and behold, was the robin swaying on a long branch of ivy, and he greeted her with a chirp.

"You showed me where the key was yesterday," she said. "You ought to show me the door today."

The robin flew on to the top of the wall and he opened his beak and sang a loud trill.

Mary Lennox had heard a great deal about Magic in her Ayah's stories, and she always said that what happened at that moment was Magic.

The wind rushed down the walk, and it was strong enough to wave the branches of the trees. Mary had stepped close to the robin, and suddenly the gust of wind swung aside some loose ivy trails, and more suddenly still she jumped toward it and caught it in her hand, because she had seen something under it. It was the knob of a door. She put her hand in her pocket, drew out the key and found it fitted the keyhole. She turned it. She was inside the secret garden.

Chapter 5

THE STRANGEST HOUSE ANYONE EVER LIVED IN

H ow still it is!" she whispered. "No wonder—I am the first person who has spoken in here for ten years."

In one or two corners there were alcoves of evergreen with stone seats or tall moss-covered urns in them.

As she came near the second of these alcoves she thought she saw something sticking out of the black earth—sharp little pale green points, and she knelt down to look at them, and sniffed the fresh scent of the damp earth. She searched about until she found a sharp piece of wood and dug and weeded out the weeds and grass around them.

"Now they look as if they could breathe," she said.

She went from place to place, and dug and weeded, until it was time to go to her midday dinner.

"Martha," she said, "If I had a little spade I could make a little garden. How much would a spade cost – a little one? Mrs. Medlock said I was to have a shilling a week to spend."

"Tha' can buy anything in th' world," said Martha. "My father only gets 16 shilling a week for the twelve of us." A shilling would be worth about ten dollars today.

"My word, that's riches! Now I've just thought of somethin'. Does tha' know how to print letters?"

"I know how to write."

"Our Dickon can only read printin'. If tha' could print we could write an' ask him to go an' buy th' garden tools an' th' seeds."

This was the letter Martha dictated to her:

My Dear Dickon:

This comes hoping to find you well as it leaves me at present. Miss Mary has plenty of money and will you go to Thwaite to buy her some flower seeds and a set of garden tools to make a flower-bed. Pick the prettiest ones and easy to grow because she has never done it before and lived in India which is different. Give my love to mother and every one of you.

Your loving sister, Martha Phoebe Sowerby

"We'll put the money in th' envelope an' I'll get the butcher's boy to take it in his cart. Dickon'll bring 'em to you himself."

The sun shone down for nearly a week on the secret garden. The secret garden was what Mary called it when she was thinking of it.

One morning she went skipping slowly down a laurel-hedged walk which curved round the secret garden and ended at a gate which opened into a wood in the park. And when she reached the little park she heard a low, peculiar whistling sound. A boy was sitting under a tree, playing on a rough wooden pipe.

When he saw Mary he held up his hand and spoke to her in a voice almost as low as and rather like his piping.

"I'm Dickon," the boy said. "I know tha'rt Miss Mary."

He did not speak to her as if they had never seen each other before but as if he knew her quite well.

"I've got th' garden tools. An' th' woman in th' shop threw in a packet o' white poppy an' one o' blue larkspur when I bought th' other seeds."

They sat down and he took a clumsy little brown paper package out of his coat pocket. "There's a lot o' mignonette an' poppies," he said. "Mignonette's th' sweetest smellin' thing as grows, an' it'll grow wherever you cast it, same as poppies will." He stopped and turned his head quickly.

"Where's that robin?"

The chirp came from a thick holly bush.

"There he is in the bush. He knows thee. He'll tell me all about thee in a minute."

He made a sound like the robin's own twitter. The robin listened a few seconds, intently, and then answered as if he were replying.

"Aye, he's a friend o' yours."

"Do you understand everything birds say?"

"I think I do, and they think I do. Where is tha' garden? Tha's got a bit o' garden, hasn't tha'?"

"I don't know—could you keep a secret?"

Dickon rubbed his hands over his rough head. "If I couldn't keep secrets from th' other lads, secrets about foxes' cubs, an' birds' nests, an' wild things' holes, there'd be naught safe on th' moor. Aye, I can keep secrets."

"I've stolen a garden. Nobody wants it, nobody cares for it. Perhaps everything is dead in it

already. I don't know. They're letting it die, all shut in by itself."

"Eh-h-h! Where is it?"

"Come with me and I'll show you."

She led him to where the ivy grew so thickly. Dickon

felt as if he were being led to look at some strange bird's nest and must move softly. When she stepped to the wall and lifted the hanging ivy, he started. There was a door and Mary pushed it slowly open and they passed in together.

Chapter 6

"MIGHT I HAVE A BIT OF EARTH?"

He stood looking round him.

"I never thought I'd see this place."

"Did you know about it?" asked Mary.

Dickon nodded.

"Will there be roses? Can you tell? I thought perhaps they were all dead."

"Eh! No! Look here!"

He took a thick knife out of his pocket.

"This here's a new bit," and he touched a shoot which looked brownish green instead of hard, dry grey.

He lifted his head to look up at the climbing and hanging sprays above him—"There'll be a fountain o' roses here this summer."

Dickon began to clear places to plant seeds, and Mary was startled and sorry when she heard the clock strike the hour of her midday dinner.

"I shall have to go. Whatever happens, you—you never would tell?"

"Not me. Tha' art as safe as a missel thrush."

A missel thrush is a large brown bird, nearly a foot long. They eat missletoe berries and protect their favorite tree from other birds during winter.

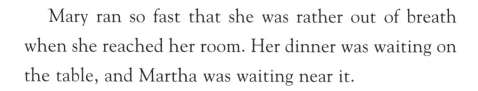

Mary ran so fast that she was rather out of breath when she reached her room. Her dinner was waiting on the table, and Martha was waiting near it.

"Tha's a bit late. Where has tha' been?"

"I've seen Dickon!"

"How does tha' like him?"

"I—I think he's beautiful!"

Mary was afraid that Martha might begin to ask difficult questions when she began to ask where the flowers were to be planted.

"Who did tha' ask about it?"

"I haven't asked anybody yet."

Mary ate her dinner and when she rose from the table, the door opened, and Mrs. Medlock walked in.

"Your hair's rough. Go and brush it. Martha, help her to slip on her best dress. Mr. Craven sent me to bring her to him in his study."

All the pink left Mary's cheeks, and after she was quite tidy she followed Mrs. Medlock down the corridors, in silence. She would not like him. She knew what he would think of her. She was taken to a part of the house she had not been into before. At last Mrs.

Medlock knocked at a door, and when someone said, "Come in," they entered the room together. A man was sitting in an armchair before the fire.

"This is Miss Mary, sir."

When she went out and closed the door, Mary could only stand waiting, a plain little thing, twisting her thin hands together. She could see that the man in the chair was not so much a hunchback as a man with high, rather crooked shoulders, and he had black hair streaked with white.

"Come here!" he said. "Are you well?"

"Yes."

"Do they take good care of you?"

"Yes."

He rubbed his forehead fretfully.

"You are very thin."

His black eyes seemed as if they scarcely saw her.

"I intended to send you a governess or a nurse, or some-one of that sort, but I forgot."

"Please," began Mary. "I am too big for a nurse. And please don't make me have a governess yet."

"What do you want to do?"

"I want to play out of doors."

"Where do you play?"

"Everywhere. I don't do any harm."

"Don't look so frightened. You could not do any harm. I sent for you to-day because Mrs. Sowerby said I ought to see you. Her daughter had talked about you. Play out of doors as much as you like. You may go where you like and amuse yourself as you like. Is there any-thing you want—toys, books, dolls?"

"Might I have a bit of earth?"

"Earth! What do you mean?"

"To plant seeds in—to make things grow—to see them come alive."

"You can have as much earth as you want. When you

see a bit of earth you want, take it, child, and make it come alive. There! You must go now, I'm tired." He touched the bell. "Good-bye. I shall be away all summer."

Mrs. Medlock came so quickly that she must have been waiting in the corridor.

"Mrs. Medlock, let her run wild in the garden. She needs liberty and fresh air and romping about."

When Mrs. Medlock left her at the end of her own corridor Mary ran to the garden, but there was no Dickon to be seen. Something white fastened to the standard rose-bush caught her eye. It was a piece of paper, fastened on the bush with a long thorn. There were some roughly printed letters on it and a sort of picture. At first she could not tell what it was. Then she saw it was meant for a nest with a bird sitting on it. Underneath, the letters said: "I will cum bak."

Chapter 7

"I AM COLIN"

Mary took the picture back to the house when she went to her supper.

"Eh!" said Martha, "That there's a picture of a missel thrush on her nest."

Then Mary knew Dickon would keep her secret. And she fell asleep looking forward to the morning.

But she was awakened in the night by the rain beating against her window, and the wind "wuthering" round the huge old house. Suddenly something made her sit up.

"That isn't the wind."

There was a candle by her bedside and she took it up and went softly out of the room. The far-off faint crying

led her. Was this the right corner? Yes, there was the tapestry door. She pushed it open very gently and closed it behind her. A few yards farther on there was a door. She could see a glimmer of light coming from beneath it. So she walked to the door and pushed it open. There was a night light burning by the side of a carved four-poster bed hung with brocade, and on the bed was lying a boy, crying fretfully.

The boy had a sharp, delicate face the color of ivory. Mary stood near the door with her candle in her hand, and he turned his head on his pillow and stared at her.

"Who are you?" he said in a half-frightened whisper. "Are you a ghost?"

"No, I am not." Mary answered. "Are you one?"

"No," he replied, "I am Colin Craven. Who are you?"

"I am Mary Lennox. Mr. Craven is my uncle."

"He is my father."

"Your father! No one ever told me he had a boy!"

"The servants are not allowed to speak about me. If I live I may be a hunchback, but I shan't live. My father hates to think I may be like him."

Mr. Craven told Colin many times that he was sick and wouldn't live, and Colin began to believe it. He would feel sick even though he was healthy. He never even learned to walk!

"Have you been locked up?"

"No. I stay in this room because I don't want to be moved. It tires me too much."

"Does your father come and see you?"

"Sometimes. Generally when I'm asleep. He doesn't want to see me."

"Why?"

"My mother died when I was born and it makes him wretched to look at me. He thinks I don't know, but I've heard people talking."

"Have you been here always?"

"Nearly always. I used to wear an iron thing to keep my back straight, but a grand doctor came from London and told them to take it off and keep me out in the fresh air. I hate fresh air and I don't want to go out."

"I didn't when I first came here," said Mary. "Why do you keep looking at me like that?"

"Because I don't want it to be a dream. If you are real, sit down on that big footstool and talk. I want to hear about you."

He made her tell him about India and about her voyage across the ocean. She found out that he could have anything he asked for and was never made to do anything he did not like to do. "It makes me ill to be angry. How old are you?" he asked.

"I am ten," answered Mary, "and so are you."

"How do you know that?"

"Because when you were born the garden door was locked and the key was buried. And it has been locked for ten years."

"What garden door? Where was the key buried?"

"It was the garden Mr. Craven hates. No one knew where he buried the key," was Mary's careful answer. But he asked question after question. Had she never asked the gardeners?

"They won't talk about it."

"I would make them," said Colin. "If I were to live, this place would sometime belong to me. They all know that."

"Do you think you won't live?" she asked.

"I don't suppose I shall. Ever since I remember anything I have heard people say I shan't."

"Do you want to live?"

"No. But I don't want to die. Let us talk about something else. That garden. I don't think I ever wanted to see something before, but I want to see that garden. I am going to make them open the door."

"Oh, don't—don't—don't do that!"

"You said you wanted to see it."

"I do," she answered "but if you make them open the door and take you in like that it will never be a secret again."

"What do you mean?"

"You see, if no one knows but ourselves—if there was a door, hidden somewhere under the ivy—and we could find it, and if we could slip through it together and shut

it behind us, and no one knew anyone was inside and
we called it our garden and if we played there almost
every day and dug and planted seeds and made it all
come alive—"

"Is it dead?" he
interrupted her.

"It soon will be
if no one cares for
it."

"I never had a
secret," he said. "I
am going to let you
look at something.
Do you see that silk
curtain over the
mantel-piece? Go
and pull it."

Mary got up and pulled the silk curtain back and
uncovered a picture of a girl with a laughing face.

"She is my mother. I don't see why she died. Sometimes I hate her for doing it."

"Her eyes are just like yours. Why is the curtain drawn over her?"

"I made them do it. Sometimes I don't like to see her looking at me. She smiles too much. Besides, she is mine and I don't want everyone to see her. I'm glad you came. I think you shall be a secret, too. Martha shall tell you when to come here."

"Shall I go away now?"

"I wish I could go to sleep before you leave me."

"Shut your eyes," said Mary. She leaned against the bed and began to sing a very low little chanting song in Hindustani.

When she looked at him again he was fast asleep. So she took her candle and crept away.

Chapter 8

A YOUNG RAJAH

When the morning came, the rain had not stopped. Martha was so busy that Mary had no opportunity of talking to her, but in the afternoon she asked her to come and sit with her.

"I have found out what the crying was. It was Colin. I found him."

Martha's face became red with fright.

"Eh! Miss Mary! Tha'll get me in trouble."

"He was glad I came. Before I left him I sang him to sleep. I think he almost liked me."

"Then tha' must have bewitched him!"

"Is Colin a hunchback?"

"He isn't yet," said Martha. "But they was afraid his back was weak an' they've always been takin' care of it—not lettin' him walk."

Very soon afterward a bell rang.

"I hope he's in a good temper."

She came back with a puzzled expression.

"Well, tha' has bewitched him. You'd better go as quick as you can."

There was a bright fire on the hearth when she entered his room, and Colin was wrapped in a velvet dressing-gown and sat against a big brocaded cushion.

"Come in," he said. "I've been thinking about you all morning."

"I've been thinking about you, too," said Mary.

"I was thinking, how different you are from Dickon."

"Who is Dickon?"

"He is Martha's brother. He is twelve years old. He can charm foxes and squirrels and birds."

Colin was actually sitting up as if he'd forgotten about his weak back, when the door opened and in walked Dr. Craven and Mrs. Medlock.

"Good Lord!" exclaimed Mrs. Medlock.

"What is this?" said Dr. Craven.

Colin answered, "This is my cousin, Mary Lennox. I asked her to come and talk to me. She must come and talk to me whenever I send for her."

Dr. Craven sat down by Colin and felt his pulse.

"I am afraid there has been too much excitement. Excitement is not good for you, my boy."

"Dr. Craven is my father's poorer cousin," Colin had told Mary. "If I die he will have all Misselthwaite after my father dies."

"He does look rather better, sir," ventured Mrs. Medlock. "But he looked better this morning before she came into the room."

"She came into the room last night. She stayed with me a long time. I was better when I wakened up. I wanted my breakfast. I want my tea now. They are always wanting me to eat things when I don't want to," said Colin, as the nurse brought in the tea. "Now, if you'll eat I will."

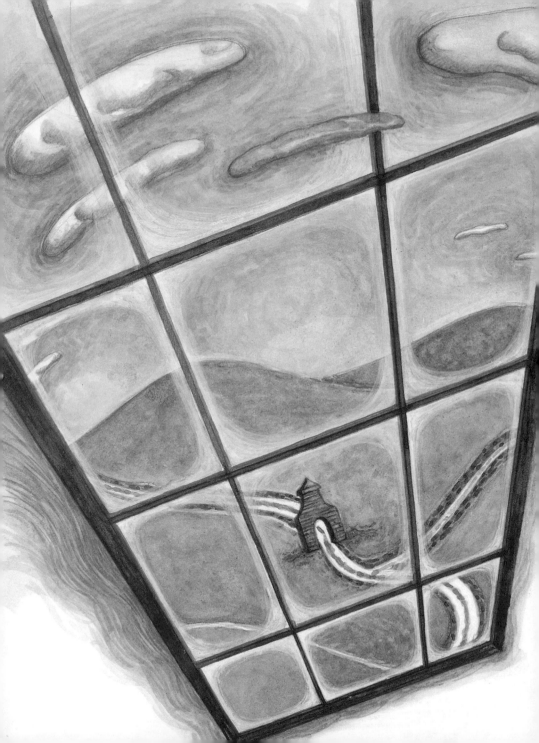

Chapter 9

NEST BUILDING

After another week of rain the blue sky appeared again. Mary wakened very early. The whole world looked as if something Magic had happened to it, and the sky was so blue and pink and pearly and flooded with springtime light that she felt as if she must sing aloud and knew that thrushes and robins and skylarks could not possibly help it. She ran around the shrubs and paths towards the secret garden.

Six months before, Mistress Mary would not have seen how the world was waking up, but now she missed nothing.

When she reached the door under the ivy, she was startled by the caw-caw of a crow from the top of the wall. He made her a little nervous, but the next moment he spread his wings and flapped away across the garden, and when she got fairly into the garden she saw that he had alighted on a dwarf apple-tree. Under the apple-tree was lying a little reddish animal with a bushy tail, and both of them were watching Dickon, who was working hard.

Mary flew across the grass to him.

"Oh, Dickon! Dickon!"

"Eh!" he said. "Th' world's all fair begun again this

mornin', it has. This is th' little fox cub," he said, rub-
bing the little reddish animal's head. "It's named
Captain. An' this here's Soot."

Swiftly something flew across the wall and darted
through the trees to a close grown corner, a little flare
of red-breasted bird with something hanging from its
beak. Dickon stood quite still and put his hands on
Mary almost as if they had suddenly found themselves
laughing in a church.

"We munnot stir. We munnot scarce breathe. It's
Ben Weatherstaff's robin. He's buildin' his nest. He'll
be a good bit different till all this is over. He'll be shyer

an' readier to take things ill. He's got no time for visitin' an' gossipin'. Us must keep still a bit an' try to look as if us was grass an' trees an' bushes. Then when he's got used to seein' us I'll chirp a bit an' he'll know us'll not be in his way."

"Do you know about Colin?" she whispered.

"Everybody as knowed about Mester Craven, knowed there was a little lad as was like to be a cripple, an' they say as Mr. Craven can't bear to see him when he's awake an' it's because his eyes is so like his mother's an' yet looks so different in his miserable bit of face."

"Do you think he wants to die?"

"No, but he wishes he'd never been born. Mester Craven, he'd buy anythin' as money could buy for th' poor lad but he's afraid he'll look at him some day and find he's growed hunchback."

"Colin's so afraid of it himself that he won't sit up," said Mary.

"Eh! When first we got in here, it seemed like everything was grey. Look around now."

Mary looked. "Why, the grey wall is changing. It is as if the green mist were creeping over it—almost like a green gauze veil."

"Aye," said Dickon. "An' if he was out here he wouldn't be watchin' for lumps to grow on his back; he'd be watchin' for buds to break on th' rose-bushes. Us'd not be thinkin' he'd better never been born. Us'd be just two children watchin' a garden grow, an' he'd be another. Two lads an' a little lass just lookin' on at th' springtime."

Mary quite forgot Colin until the sun was sending deep gold rays slanting under the trees.

She ran back to the house, to see Martha waiting for her.

"Eh! He was nigh goin' into one of his tantrums. There's been a nice to-do all afternoon to keep him quiet."

Mary's lips pinched themselves together. When she went into his room, he was lying flat on his back in bed and he did not turn his head towards her as she came in. Mary marched up to him with her stiff manner.

"Why didn't you get up?"

"I did get up this morning when I thought you were coming," he answered. "I made them put me back in bed this afternoon. My back ached and my head ached and I was tired. And I won't let that boy come here if you go and stay with him instead of coming to talk to me."

"If you send Dickon away, I'll never come into this room again!" she retorted.

"You'll have to if I want you."

"I won't!"

"I'll make you. They shall drag you in."

"Shall they! They may drag me in but they can't make me talk when they get me here. I won't even look at you!"

"You are a selfish thing!" cried Colin.

"What are you?" said Mary. "Selfish people always say that. You're the most selfish boy I ever saw."

"I'm not as selfish as your fine Dickon is!"

"He's nicer than any boy that ever lived!"

Colin shut his eyes and a big tear was squeezed out and ran down his cheek.

"I'm not as selfish as you, because I'm always ill, and I'm sure

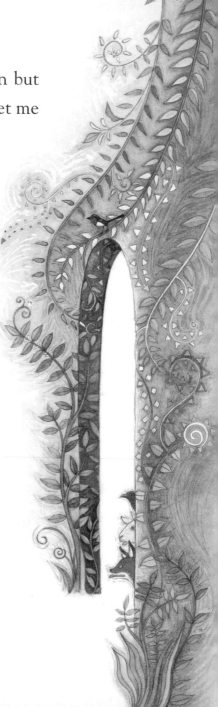

there is a lump coming on my back. And I am going to die besides."

"You're not!"

"I'm not? I am! Everybody says so."

"You just say that to make people sorry."

"Get out of the room!" he shouted.

"I'm going," she said. "And I won't come back!" She walked to the door and when she reached it she turned round.

"I was going to tell you all sorts of nice things," she said. "Dickon brought his fox and his rook and I was going to tell you all about them. Now I won't tell you a single thing!"

The rook was the crow Mary saw in the garden, a big glossy-plumaged blue-black bird, on top of the wall, looking down wisely at her.

She marched out of the door and went back to her room.

Chapter 10

A TANTRUM

Martha was waiting for her. There was a wooden box on the table full of neat packages.

"Mr. Craven sent it to you," said Martha.

There were several beautiful books, and two of them were about gardens and full of pictures. There were two or three games and a beautiful little writing-case and a gold pen and inkstand. Everything was so nice; she had not expected him to remember her at all.

"The first thing I shall write with that pen will be a letter to tell him I am much obliged."

She had got up very early, so as soon as Martha had

brought her supper and she had eaten it, she was glad to go to bed.

She thought it was the middle of the night when she was wakened by such dreadful sounds that she jumped out of bed in an instant.

As she listened to the sobbing screams she put her hands over her ears and felt sick, and suddenly they began to make her angry. She stamped her foot.

"Somebody ought to make him stop!" she cried out.

Just then her door opened and the nurse came in.

"He's worked himself into hysterics," she said in a great hurry. "No one can do anything with him. You're in the right humor, you go and scold him. Give him something new to think of."

Mary thought it was funny that the grown-ups asked her to help with Colin because they guessed she was almost as bad as Colin himself.

Mary flew along the corridor. She felt quite wicked by the time she reached the door. She slapped it open with her hand.

"You stop, I hate you."

"I can't stop! I can't—I can't!"

"You can!"

"I felt the lump—I felt it. I shall have a hunch on my back and then I shall die."

"You didn't. It was only a hysterical lump. There's nothing the matter with your horrid back! Nurse, come here and show me his back!"

"There's not a single lump there!" she said at last. "If you ever say there is again, I shall laugh!"

"I didn't know," ventured the nurse, "that he thought he had a lump on his spine. His back is weak because he won't try to sit up. I could have told him there was no lump there."

"Could you?" he said.

"Yes, sir."

"Do you think—I could—live to grow up?"

"You probably will if you will not give way to your temper, and stay out in the fresh air."

Colin put out his hand a little toward Mary.

"I'll go out with you, Mary," he said, "I do so want to see Dickon and the fox and the crow."

"I will put him to sleep," Mary said to the yawning nurse.

As soon as she was gone Colin pulled Mary's hand.

"I almost told," he said, "but I stopped myself in time. Have you—do you think you have found out anything at all about the way into the secret garden?"

"Ye-es, I think I have. And if you will go to sleep I will tell you tomorrow."

"Oh, Mary! Do you suppose that instead of singing the Ayah song you could just tell me softly as you did that first day what you imagine it looks like inside?"

"Yes. Shut your eyes. I think it has been left alone so long—that it has grown all into a lovely tangle. I think the roses have climbed and climbed until they hang from the branches and walls and creep over the ground—almost like a strange grey mist. Some of them have died but many are alive and when the summer comes there will be curtains and fountains of roses. I think the ground is full of daffodils and snowdrops and lilies and iris working their way out of the dark. Now the spring has begun—perhaps they are coming up through the grass—perhaps there are clusters of purple crocuses and gold ones—even now. And perhaps the robin has found a mate—and is building a nest."

And Colin was asleep.

Chapter 11

"THA' MUNNOT WASTE NO TIME"

Next morning, when Martha brought her breakfast she told her that Colin was feverish.

"Eh! Poor lad! He's been spoiled till salt won't save him. But he says to me, 'Please ask Miss Mary if she'll please come an' talk to me.'"

Martha's mother had told her the two worst things that could happen to a child were to never have his own way—or to always have it, and be spoiled. Sometimes salt could keep food from spoiling, but nothing would save a spoiled child.

She had her hat on when she appeared in Colin's room and for a second he looked disappointed.

"Are you going somewhere?"

"I won't be long, I'm going to Dickon, but I'll come back. Colin, it's—it's something about the garden."

"Oh! Is it?" he cried out. "I dreamed about it all night."

In five minutes Mary was with Dickon in their garden. The fox and the crow were with him again and this time he had brought two tame squirrels.

"I came over on the pony this mornin'," he said. "Eh! He is a good little chap, Jump is! I brought these two in my pockets. This one here's called Nut an' this here other one's called Shell."

When he said "Nut" one squirrel leaped on to his right shoulder and when he said "Shell" the other one leaped on his left shoulder.

They sat down on the grass, but when she began to tell her story she could see he felt sorrier for Colin than she did.

"Eh! My! We mun get him out here—we mun get him watchin' an listenin' an' sniffin' up th' air an' get him just soaked through wi' sunshine. An' we munnot lose no time about it."

It was hard to go, particularly as Nut had actually crept on to her dress. But she went back to the house and when she sat down close to Colin's bed he began to sniff as Dickon did.

"You smell like flowers and—and fresh things. What is it you smell of?"

"It's th' wind from th' moor. It's th' springtime an' out o' doors an' sunshine as smells so graidely."

Mary was quite proud of herself, having learned to speak Yorkshire like Dickon and Martha, and saying "graidely" instead of "fine."

Colin began to laugh.

"What are you doing?"

"Doesn't tha' understand a bit o' Yorkshire when tha' hears it? An' tha' a Yorkshire lad thysel' bred an' born! Eh! I wonder tha'rnt ashamed o' thy face."

And then she began to laugh too and they both laughed until they could not stop themselves.

There was so much to talk about. Mary had run round into the wood with Dickon to see Jump. He was a tiny little shaggy moor pony with thick locks hanging over his eyes. Dickon had talked into his ear and Jump had talked back in odd little whinnies and puffs and snorts.

"Does he really understand everything Dickon says?" Colin asked.

"Dickon says anything will understand if you're friends with it for sure."

Colin lay quiet.

"I wish I was friends with things," he said at last,

"but I'm not. I never had anything to be friends with, and I can't bear people."

Mary caught hold of both his hands.

"Can I trust you? I trusted Dickon because birds trusted him. Can I trust you—for sure?"

"Yes—yes!"

"Well, Dickon will come to see you tomorrow morning. But that's not all. There is a door into the garden. I found it."

"Oh! Mary! Shall I see it? Shall I live to get into it?"

"Of course you'll see it!" snapped Mary. "Of course you'll live to get into it! Don't be silly!"

And Colin began to laugh at himself.

That night Colin slept without once awakening and when he opened his eyes in the morning he lay still and smiled without knowing it. And he had not been awake more than ten minutes when he heard feet running along the corridor and Mary was at the door.

"It has come! I thought it had come that other morning, but it was only coming. It is here now! It has come, the Spring!"

"Has it?" cried Colin. "Open the window!"

"That's fresh air," she said. "Lie on your back and draw in long breaths of it. Things are crowding up out of the earth, and there are primroses in the lanes and woods, and the seeds we planted are up, and Dickon has brought the fox and the crow and the squirrels and a new-born lamb."

When the nurse entered, she started a little at the sight of the open window.

"Are you sure you are not chilly, Master Colin?"

"No, I am breathing in long breaths of fresh air. My cousin will have breakfast with me."

When Colin was on his sofa and the breakfast for two was put upon the table he made an announcement to the nurse in his most Rajah-like manner.

"A boy, and a fox, and a crow, and two squirrels, and a new-born lamb, are coming to see me this morning. I want them brought upstairs as soon as they come. The boy is Martha's brother. His name is Dickon."

"You are not to begin playing with the animals in the servants' hall," said Colin to the nurse. "I want them here."

He was not long in coming.

"If you please, sir," announced Martha, opening the door, "here's Dickon an' his creatures."

Dickon came in smiling his nicest wide smile. The new-born lamb was in his arms and the little red fox trotted by his side. Nut sat on his left shoulder and Soot on his right and Shell's head and paws peeped out of his coat pocket.

Colin slowly sat up and stared, overwhelmed by his own curiosity.

But Dickon did not feel the least shy. Creatures were always like that until they found out about you. He walked over to Colin's sofa and put the new-born lamb quietly on his lap, and immediately the little creature turned to the warm velvet dressing-gown and began to nuzzle into its folds and butt its tight-curled head with soft impatience against his side.

"What is it doing? What does it want?"

Dickon knelt down and took a feeding-bottle from his pocket.

"Come on, little 'un," he said, turning the small woolly white head with a gentle brown hand and he pushed the rubber tip of the bottle into the nuzzling mouth and the lamb began to suck it with ravenous ecstasy.

Chapter 12

"I Shall Live Forever— and Ever—and Ever!"

The most absorbing thing was the preparations to be made before Colin could be transported with sufficient secrecy to the garden. No one must ever suspect that they had a secret; and they had long talks about their route.

They would go round among the flower beds as if they were looking for the plants that Mr. Roach, the head gardener, had been having arranged. No one would think it at all mysterious.

Rumors of the new and curious things which were occurring in the invalid's apartments had of course filtered through the servants' hall but notwithstanding this, Mr. Roach was startled when he received orders that he must report himself in the apartment no outsider had ever seen.

"Things are changing in this house, Mr. Roach," said Mrs. Medlock, as she led him up the back staircase.

"Here is Mr. Roach, Master Colin," said Mrs. Medlock.

"Oh, you are Roach, are you?" he said. "I sent for you to give you some very important orders. I am going out in my chair this afternoon," said Colin. "If the fresh air agrees with me I may go out every day. When I go, none of the gardeners are to be anywhere near the Long Walk by the garden walls. No one is to be there."

"Very good, sir," replied Mr. Roach.

Dickon went back to the garden, and Mary stayed with Colin.

A little later the nurse made Colin ready. She noticed that instead of lying like a log while his clothes were put on he sat up and made some efforts to help himself.

The strongest footman in the house carried Colin downstairs and put him in his wheeled chair. Dickon began to push the chair, and Colin leaned back and lifted his

face to the sky. At last they turned into the Long Walk by the ivied walls.

"This is it," breathed Mary.

"Is it?" cried Colin. "But I can see nothing. There is no door."

"That's what I thought," and she took hold of the hanging green curtain.

Colin dropped back against his cushions, and covered his eyes with his hands and held them there until they were inside and the chair stopped and the door was closed. Not till then did he take them away and look round, and round, and round.

"I shall get well! I shall get well!" he cried out. "Mary! Dickon! I shall get well! And I shall live forever and ever and ever!"

Mary and Dickon worked a little here and there. They brought him things to look at—buds which were opening, buds which were tight closed, bits of twig whose leaves were just showing green, the feather of a woodpecker which had dropped on the grass, the empty shell of some bird early hatched.

The afternoon was dragging towards its mellow hour. The bees were going home, the birds were flying past less often, and Colin was lying against his cushions.

"I don't want this afternoon to go," he said, "but I shall come back tomorrow, and the day after, and the day after."

"That tha' will," said Dickon. "Us'll have thee walkin' about here an' diggin' same as other folk afore long."

Colin flushed.

"Walk!" he said. "Dig! Shall I?"

"For sure tha' will. Tha's got legs o' thine own, same as other folks!"

"Nothing really ails them," Colin answered, "but they shake so that I'm afraid to try to stand on them."

"When tha' stops bein' afraid tha'lt stand on 'em. An' tha'lt stop bein' afraid in a bit."

"I shall?" said Colin. "Who is that man?" Dickon and Mary scrambled to their feet.

There was Ben Weatherstaff's indignant face glaring at them over the wall from the top of a ladder! He shook his fist at Mary.

"I never thowt much o' thee! I couldna' abide thee th' first time I set eyes on thee. A scrawny buttermilk-faced young besom, allus askin' questions an' pokin' tha' nose where it wasna' wanted. I never knowed how tha' got so thick wi' me, tha' young nowt. However in the world did tha' get in?"

"It was the robin who showed me the way."

Ben Weatherstaff stopped shaking his fist very suddenly at that very moment and his jaw actually dropped as he stared over her head at a wheeled chair with luxurious cushions and robes, which came toward him looking rather like some sort of State Coach. A young Rajah leaned back in it with royal command in his great black-rimmed eyes and a thin white hand extended haughtily towards him.

"Do you know who I am?"

"Who tha' art? Aye, that I do—wi' tha' mother's eyes starin' at me out o' tha' face. Lord knows how tha' came here. But tha'rt th' poor cripple."

Colin flushed and sat bolt upright.

"I'm not a cripple! I'm not!"

"Tha' hasn't got a crooked back?"

"No!"

"Tha' hasn't got crooked legs?"

It was too much. Never yet had he been accused of crooked legs—even in whispers.

"Come here!" he shouted to Dickon.

Mary caught her breath: "He can do it! He can do it! He can do it! He can!" she gabbled over to herself as fast as she could.

There was a brief fierce scramble, the rugs were tossed on the ground, Dickon held Colin's arm, the thin legs were out, the thin feet were on the grass. Colin was standing upright—as straight as an arrow and looking strangely tall—his head thrown back.

"Look at me! Just look at me—you!"

"He's as straight as I am!" cried Dickon. "He's as straight as any lad in Yorkshire!"

Ben Weatherstaff choked and gulped and suddenly tears ran down his weather-wrinkled cheeks as he struck his old hands together.

"Eh! Th' lies folks tells! Tha'rt as thin as a lath an' as white as a wraith, but there's not a knob on thee. Tha'lt make a mon yet. God bless thee!"

"You get down from that ladder and go out to the

Long Walk and Miss Mary will meet you and bring you here. I want to talk to you."

When his head was out of sight Mary flew across the grass to the door under the ivy. Dickon was watching with sharp eyes.

"I'm going to walk to that tree. I'm going to be standing when Weatherstaff comes."

When Ben Weatherstaff came through the door in the wall he heard Mary muttering something under her breath. Colin fixed his eyes on Ben Weatherstaff.

"Look at me! Am I a hunchback? Have I got crooked legs?"

"Not tha'," he said. "What's tha' been doin' with thysel'—hidin' out o' sight an' lettin' folks think tha' was cripple an' half-witted?"

"Half-witted?"

"What did tha' shut thyself up for?"

"Everyone thought I was going to die. I'm not!"

Ben Weatherstaff looked him over.

"Tha' die! Tha's got too much pluck in thee. When I seed thee put tha' legs on th' ground in such a hurry I knowed tha' was all right. Sit thee down on th' rug a bit young Mester, an' give me thy orders."

"What work do you do in the gardens, Weatherstaff?"

"Anythin' I'm told to do. I'm kep' on by favor—because she liked me."

"She?"

"Tha' mother."

"My mother? This was her garden, wasn't it?"

"Aye, it was that!"

"It is my garden now. I shall come here every day. But it is to be a secret. My orders are that no one is to know that we come here. I shall send for you sometimes to help—but you must come when no one can see you."

"I've come here before when no one saw me."

"But no one has been in it for ten years!" cried Colin. "There was no door!"

"I'm no one," said old Ben dryly. "An' I didn't come through th' door. I come over th' wall. Th' rheumatics held me back th' last two years. She says to me once, 'Ben, if ever I'm ill or I go away you must take care of my roses.' When she did go away th' orders was no one was ever to come nigh. But I come. Over th' wall I come, once a year. She'd gave her order first. It'll be easier wi' rheumatics to come in at th' door."

"How'd tha' like to plant something?" Forgetting rheumatics, Ben brought a rose in a pot from the greenhouse. He knelt by the hole Colin had dug, ignoring the ache in his joints, and helped him settle the plant in the earth.

Chapter 13

MAGIC

They always called it Magic and indeed it seemed like it in the months that followed. Iris and white lilies rose out of the grass in sheaths, and the green alcoves filled themselves with tall delphiniums or columbines. And the roses, rising out of the grass, came alive day by day. Colin saw it all. Every morning he was brought out and every hour of each day when it didn't rain he spent in the garden.

Even on gray days, Colin would lie on the grass "watching things growing," he said. If you watched long enough, he declared, you could see buds unsheathe themselves.

He sent for Ben Weatherstaff.

"Good morning, Ben Weatherstaff," he said. "I want you and Dickon and Miss Mary to stand in a row and listen to me because I am going to tell you something very important. When I grow up I am going to make great scientific discoveries and I am going to begin now. The great scientific discoveries I am going to make will be about Magic. I'm sure there is Magic in everything, only we have not sense enough to get hold of it and make it do things for us—like electricity and horses and steam. The Magic in this garden has made me stand up and know I am going to live to be a man. When I was going to try to stand that first time Mary kept saying to herself as fast as she could, 'You can do

it! You can do it!' and I did. I had to try at the same time, of course, but her Magic helped me—and so did Dickon's."

Colin suggested that they should all sit cross-legged under the tree, and it all seemed most majestic and mysterious when they sat down in their circle. Colin held his head high like a sort of priest.

"Now we shall begin."

And he began: "The sun is shining—the sun is shining. That is the Magic. The flowers are growing—the roots are stirring. That is the Magic. Being alive is the Magic—being strong is the Magic. The Magic is in

me—the Magic is in me. It is in every one of us. Magic! Magic! Come and help!"

"Now I am going to walk round the garden," he announced.

Colin leaned on Dickon's arm, but now and then he took his hand from its support and walked a few steps alone.

"The Magic is in me!" he kept saying. "The Magic is making me strong! I can feel it! I can feel it!"

He sat on the seats in the alcoves, and once or twice he sat down on the grass, but he would not give up until he had gone all round the garden. When he returned his cheeks were flushed.

"I did it! The Magic worked! That is my first scientific discovery."

"What will Dr. Craven say?" broke out Mary.

"He won't say anything," Colin answered, "because he will not be told. This is to be secret. I shall come here every day in my chair and I shall be taken back in it. I won't let my father hear about it until the experiment has quite succeeded. Then sometime, when he comes back to Misselthwaite, I shall just walk into his study and say 'Here I am; I am like any other boy. I am quite well and I shall live to be a man. It has been done by a scientific experiment.'"

"He will think he is in a dream," cried Mary. "He won't believe his eyes."

Colin had made himself believe that he was going to get well, which was really more than half the battle. He imagined what his father would look like when he saw his son as straight and strong as other fathers' sons.

One afternoon, Mary noticed that something new had happened in Colin's room. She said nothing, but she sat and looked at the picture over the mantel.

"I know what you want me to tell you," said Colin.

"You are wondering why the curtain is drawn back. I am going to keep it like that."

"Why?"

"Because it doesn't make me angry any more to see her laughing. I wakened when it was bright moonlight two nights ago and felt as if the Magic was filling the room and I couldn't lie still. The room was quite light and there was a patch of moonlight on the curtain and somehow that made me go and pull the cord. She looked right down at me as if she were laughing because she was glad I was standing there. I want to see her laughing like that all the time. I think she must have been a sort of Magic person perhaps."

After the morning's incantations Colin sometimes gave them Magic lectures.

"I like to do it," he explained, "because when I grow up and make great scientific discoveries I shall be obliged to lecture about them and so this is practice."

It was not very long after he had said this that he laid down his trowel and stretched himself out to his tallest height and threw out his arms.

"Now that I am a real boy," Colin had said, "my legs and arms and all my body are so full of Magic that I can't keep them still. They want to be doing things all the time."

"Mary! Dickon! Just this minute, all at once I remembered—and I had to stand up on my feet to see if it was real. And it is real! I'm well—I'm well! I shall live for ever and ever! I shall find thousands and thousands of things. And I shall never stop making Magic—I feel as if I want to shout out something—something thankful, joyful!"

Chapter 14

IN THE GARDEN

While the secret garden was coming to life, there was a man wandering the Norwegian fjords and the valleys and mountains of Switzerland, who for ten years had kept his mind filled with dark and heartbroken thinking. Until one day, when he was in the Austrian Tyrol, Archibald Craven gradually felt his mind and body grow as quiet as the valley itself. Something seemed to have been unbound and released in him, very quietly.

Months afterward he found out quite by accident that it was on this very day Colin had cried out as he went into the secret garden: "I am going to live forever and ever and ever!"

As summer changed into golden autumn he went to Lake Como, and one day he had walked so far that when he returned the moon was high and he walked down to a little bowered terrace at the water's edge. He felt the strange calmness stealing over him.

He did not know when he fell asleep and when he began to dream. He thought he heard a voice calling. "Archie!" it said, "Archie! Archie!"

"Lilias!" he answered. "Where are you?"

"In the garden."

And then the dream ended.

He slept soundly and sweetly all night. When he did awake at last a servant was standing staring at him. The man held a salver with some letters on

it. When he glanced at the letters a few minutes later he saw that the one lying at the top of the rest came from Yorkshire. He opened it.

Dear Sir:

I am Susan Sowerby that made bold to speak to you once on the moor. It was about Miss Mary I spoke. I will make bold to speak again. Please, sir, I would come home if I was you. I think you would be glad to come and—if you will excuse me, sir—I think your lady would ask you to come if she was here.

Your obedient servant, Susan Sowerby.

Mr. Craven read the letter twice before he put it back in its envelope.

In a few days he was in Yorkshire again, and when he arrived at the Manor he took his way through the door in the shrubbery, crossed the lawn and turned into the Long Walk by the ivied walls.

He had not meant to be a bad father, but he had not felt like a father at all. He had shrunk from the mere thought of the boy and had buried himself in his own misery. "Perhaps I have been all wrong for ten years," he said. "It may be too late."

The ivy hung thick over the door, and yet inside the garden there were sounds—exclamations and smothered joyous cries. Was he losing his reason?

And then the feet ran faster and faster, nearing the garden door. There was quick strong young breathing and a wild outbreak of laughing—and the door in the wall was flung open, the sheet of ivy swinging back, and a boy burst through it and, without seeing the outsider, dashed almost into his arms. Mr. Craven held him away to look at him.

There were the sounds of running scuffling feet seeming to chase round and round under the trees, sounds of lowered suppressed voices, exclamations and smothered joyous cries.

"Father! I'm Colin."

"In the garden!"

"Yes, it was the garden that did it—and Mary and Dickon and the Magic."

Mr. Craven put his hands on both the boy's shoulders and held him still.

"Take me into the garden, my boy," he said at last. "And tell me all about it."

And so they led him in. The place was a wilderness of autumn gold and purple and violet blue and flaming scarlet and on every side were sheaves of late lilies standing

together—white or white and ruby. Late
roses climbed and hung and clustered.
He looked round and round.

"I thought it would be dead," he said.

"Mary thought so at first," said
Colin. "But it came alive."

Then they sat down under
their tree—all but Colin, who
wanted to stand while he told
the story.

KING ARTHUR
AND THE KNIGHTS OF THE ROUND TABLE

Benedict Flynn

Told by Sean Bean

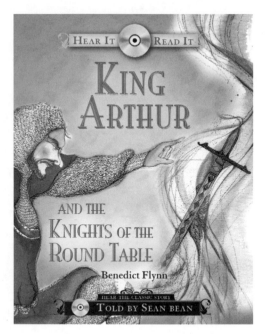

In *King Arthur and the Knights of the Round Table*, young Arthur is as surprised as anyone the day he pulls the mysterious sword from the stone and becomes the king of England! The wizard Merlin leads him to assemble his knights, including brave Sir Lancelot and pure Sir Galahad. Arthur and his knights undertake many quests to bring peace to the kingdom, and uphold justice for all. But all the while, the evil Morgana le Fay and Mordred plot to overthrow Arthur and rule themselves. Soon Arthur enters a terrible battle . . . for his kingdom, and his life.

$9.95 U.S/$11.95 CAN/£6.99 UK   ISBN-13: 978-1-4022-1243-7
ISBN-10: 1-4022-1243-7